Moon Sandwich Mom

WRITTEN BY **Jennifer Richard Jacobson**

ILLUSTRATED BY **Benrei Huang**

Albert Whitman & Company

Morton Grove, Illinois

For Erik, who reminds me to play.
—J. R. J.

For my sister Barbara,
who is also a wonderful mom.
—B. H.

Library of Congress Cataloging-in-Publication Data
Jacobson, Jennifer Richard, 1958-
Moon sandwich mom / by Jennifer Richard Jacobson ; illustrated by Benrei Huang.
p. cm.
Summary: When his mother is too busy to play with him,
Rafferty Fox sets off to find a new mother, but though others are fun sometimes,
he decides that he likes his own mother the best.
ISBN 0-8075-4071-4
[1. Mother and child–Fiction. 2. Foxes–Fiction. 3. Animals–Fiction.]
I. Huang, Benrei, ill. II. Title.
PZ7.J1529Mo 1999
[E]–dc21
98-36352
CIP
AC

The design is by Scott Piehl.

"When can you play?" asked Rafferty.
"Not now," said Mrs. Fox. "My grapes need more purple. My leaves need more green. I want to finish my painting."

"You're no fun," said Rafferty. "You never play. All you do is paint."

Mrs. Fox did not answer. She stepped back and looked at her painting for a moment. Then she added another leaf.

"I'm leaving," said Rafferty. "I'm going to find a new mother. A mother who's fun."

"All right," said Mrs. Fox. She was looking for the best orange for the color of a sunset.

Rafferty packed his baseball sweatshirt, some yellow socks, and his favorite rock. "Good-bye," he said.

"Don't go past the woods," said Mrs. Fox.

Rafferty had just reached the old oak tree when he met his friend Oswald. "Where are you going?" asked Oswald.

"To find a new mother," said Rafferty. "A mother who's fun."

"*My* mother is fun," said Oswald. "She plays lots of games. You can live with us."

Good. I have a new mother, thought Rafferty, and off he went to live with the Porcupine family.

Rafferty had fun playing badminton and T-ball, freeze tag and horseshoes. But at lunchtime, Mrs. Porcupine gave Rafferty a sandwich that was cut in half. The long way.

Rafferty's mother cut sandwiches into stars, clouds, suns, and moons. Eating lunch at the Porcupines' house was no fun at all. So Rafferty said "thank you very much" and left.

Down by the pond, Rafferty found Amanda building
a tent with sticks.

"I'm searching for a new mother," said Rafferty.

"What's wrong with your old mother?" asked Amanda.

"She isn't fun," said Rafferty.

"*My* mother's fun," said Amanda. "She can build all
sorts of things."

When Mrs. Beaver returned with a new load of sticks, Rafferty
decided to stay. All afternoon, the Beavers and Rafferty made
things. They built tents and tree houses, rockets and rafts.

Then Mrs. Beaver said, "Rest time." She told everyone to lie down while she watched her show on television. She didn't read to them. Not one book.

Rafferty's mother always read to him while he rested. She sang lullabies, too. Rest time was not fun at the Beavers' house. So Rafferty said "thank you for building with me" and went on his way.

"Where are you going?" asked Jerry, who was snacking on berries.

"To find a mother who's fun," said Rafferty.

"*My* mother's fun," said Jerry. "She's teaching us to play cards."

Rafferty decided he would like to learn to play cards, too. He and Jerry and the rest of the Raccoons played Crazy Eights and Old Maid, Go Fish and Slapjack. When the youngest got tired of playing and decided to see how far the cards would fly, Mrs. Raccoon said, "Bath time."

She put them all in the tub and told them to scrub.
Bath time sure was crowded at the Raccoons'. There
was no room for sailboats or submarines. There was
no room for sponges or silly foam.

Rafferty's mother hid toys under the foamy waves. She helped Rafferty make bubbly lemonade, and she always pretended to drink some. Bath time was not fun at the Raccoons'. Rafferty hopped out of the tub, said his thank yous, and left.

Soon Rafferty was back in front of his own house. He could hear his mother humming inside. He wondered what she was doing. He went up to the front window, stood on his tiptoes, and put his nose to the glass.

Mrs. Fox was looking out the window. She saw Rafferty and ran to open the door. "There you are!" she said. "I've missed you!" She gave him a big squeeze.

"Would you like to paint?"

Rafferty wrinkled his nose. Not painting again!

Mrs. Fox put her paint pots on the floor. She dipped her paws and Rafferty's paws in the paint.

They made purple tracks the color of grapes, green tracks the color of leaves, and orange tracks the color of the sunset all across the floor.

They giggled until their bellies hurt. Then they had supper.
"This is the most fun I've had all day," said Rafferty.
"Me, too," said Mrs. Fox. "Here—have a moon."

Suddenly, Rafferty's mother looked just like new.
He decided to keep her.